In memory of

Joyce Lee Bumpus

who loved cats

2011

My Cat, Coon Cat

Published by

Islandport Press

P.O. Box 10

Yarmouth, Maine 04096

www.islandportpress.com

books@islandportpress.com

Production Date: 01/11/11

Plant & Location: Printed by Everbest Printing Co. Ltd, Nansha China

Job / Batch #: 99189

ISBN: 978-1-934031-32-2

Library of Congress Control Number: 2010919363

ISLANDPORT PRESS   YARMOUTH • MAINE

My Cat,

WRITTEN BY
Sandy Ferguson Fuller

Coon Cat

ILLUSTRATIONS BY
Jeannie Brett

Hi cat, coon cat,
Heard you at the door...
Brought a mouse to our new house?
Did you live here before?

New cat, coon cat,
Do you need a home?
Would you like to be with me
Or live free on your own?

Here cat, coon cat,
Do you have a name?
If I whistle will you come?
Are you wild or tame?

Morning cat, coon cat,
Hungry for a treat?
Bowl of milk? Dish of fish?
What do you like to eat?

Noon cat, coon cat,
Lazy all the day.
Catching catnaps in the sun.
Please wake up and play!

Smooth cat, coon cat,
Very cool and classy.
My kitten's name is Marmalade.
She's a little sassy.

Shy cat, coon cat,
This dog wants some fun.
BOW-WOW-WOW!
MEEEE-OW! MEEEE-OW!

WOW! You'd better run!

Neighbor cat, coon cat,
Looks a lot like you.
Henry is humongous!
Is he a Maine coon too?

Quiet cat, coon cat,
Through the field you creep,

Shadowing a dragonfly.
Ready ... set ... leap!

Soft cat, coon cat,
Your fur is thick and warm,
So you can play hide and seek
Outside when there's a storm.

Brave cat, coon cat,
How you love the night!
The crying loon, a bright full moon,
Shadows in the light.

Evening cat, coon cat,
Purring at my head.
Be polite and try to sleep,
And you can share my bed.

Tiger Cat, how is that?
Now you have a name!
I've never had a friend like you.
I'm so glad you came!

My cat, coon cat.
GOOD NIGHT!

ABOUT MAINE COON CATS

No one knows the exact history of the Maine coon cat.
Some people believe that long haired cats from Europe,
like Persians, Angoras, or Norwegian forest cats, came by
ship to New England and bred with domestic cats. One
legend tells of a Wiscasset ship captain rescuing cats for
Marie Antoinette; another has a ship captain named Coon
bringing long-haired cats across the ocean. Whatever its
origin, this gentle and loyal cat is known for its long shaggy
coat, fluffy tail, tufted ears, and wide tufted feet. Because
it is thought to be native to Maine and is so well equipped
for cold New England winters, in 1985 the legislature
made it the State Cat of Maine! Only two other states
(Massachusetts and Maryland) have a State Cat.

ABOUT THE AUTHOR

Sandy Ferguson Fuller has indulged her entire professional life in the fun world of children's books, originally inspired as a student of Maurice Sendak's at Yale. Her work requires wearing many hats, including picture book author, illustrator, literary agent, bookseller, and publishing consultant. Her agency, Alp Arts Co., represents such well-known authors as John Denver, Carmela LaVigna Coyle, Dylan Pritchett, Robert Baldwin, Pattie Schnetzler, and Anthony D. Fredericks. When she's not creating or selling books, she often can be found looking for loons on her favorite Maine lake, or hiking up and skiing down her native Colorado mountains. Her other books include *Moon Loon*, *Out In The Night*, *Hannah And The Perfect Picture Pony*, and *The BLUES Go Birding* series. She's also the proud mom of adult kids, Scott and Kimberly, a golden retriever, Riva Girl, and once upon a time, a coon cat named Tiger!

ABOUT THE ILLUSTRATOR

Jeannie Brett has previously illustrated four children's books for Michigan-based Sleeping Bear Press: *L is for Lobster*, *A Maine Alphabet*; *Fishing for Numbers*, *A Maine Numbers Book*; *M is for Mayflower*, *A Massachusetts Alphabet*; and *One if by Land*, *A Massachusetts Numbers Book*. She also has written and illustrated *Little Maine* and illustrated *Little New York* and *Little Pennsylvania*, state-themed board books of rhyming riddles. Brett has lived in Maine for more than three decades. She attended the School of the Museum of Fine Arts, Boston and Minneapolis College of Art and Design. Brett enjoys spending her free time with her family and pets. She also enjoys visiting schoolchildren to share her love of nature, animals, art, and books!

Other children's books by Islandport Press

The Fish House Door
by Robert F. Baldwin, illustrated by Astrid Sheckels

The Scallop Christmas
by Jane Freeberg, illustrated by Astrid Sheckels

At One
by Lynn Plourde, illustrated by Leslie Mansmann

Titus Tidewater
by Suzy Verrier

Dahlov Ipcar's Farmyard Alphabet
by Dahlov Ipcar

The Calico Jungle
by Dahlov Ipcar

The Cat at Night
by Dahlov Ipcar

My Wonderful Christmas Tree
by Dahlov Ipcar

Hardscrabble Harvest
by Dahlov Ipcar

The Little Fisherman
by Margaret Wise Brown, illustrated by Dahlov Ipcar

ISLANDPORT PRESS